THiRTY BUCKS

To: Arianna and Danya Klinck,
I hope you enjoy the book!
Donita

DONITA WIEBE-NEUFELD

illustrated by Chad Thompson

Love Nana Klinck
Christmas 2015

FriesenPress

Suite 300 - 990 Fort St
Victoria, BC, Canada, V8V 3K2
www.friesenpress.com

Copyright © 2015 by Donita Wiebe-Neufeld
First Edition — 2015

Thirty Bucks is a work of fiction. The characters
and situations come from the imagination of the
author and are not meant to depict any particular
individual...except for the cat. "Thirty Bucks"
bears a remarkable likeness to the author's pet
cat, "Aphid", who is also an escape artist!

ISBN
978-1-4602-5582-7 (Paperback)
978-1-4602-5583-4 (eBook)

1. Juvenile Fiction, Holidays &
Celebrations, Christmas & Advent

Distributed to the trade by The
Ingram Book Company

A STORY OF CELEBRATION AND THANKSGIVING!

FOR TIM, WHO MADE THIS DREAM POSSIBLE.

THERE ONCE WAS A MAN living in a little white house

where the curtains were always drawn. Every day a grey car left the garage at 5:30 am and returned at 5:30 pm. In the winter, his walks were shoveled precisely to the property line, but not a centimeter beyond. Every Saturday in summer, his lawnmower growled at 7:00 am, unless it rained. All year round, a sign on the door said no soliciting, and the porch light was always off.

This man, known as Mr. Hermit by us kids, lived on my street. We didn't know anything about him. He had been there forever, like one of the big elm trees out front. His place was quiet and neat and dark, so no one bothered him.

That's how it was a couple of days before Christmas the year when the street lights quit working. Other than a few places with Christmas lights, our street was black. It was especially dark at Mr. Hermit's. His house seemed to huddle in the snow and disappear, except for a thin blue flicker of TV light seeping through the curtains.

ON THIS ONE CHRISTMAS EVE, however, Mr. Hermit's

porch light was on. Maybe it was his way of being festive, or maybe he just bumped into the light switch. Whatever happened, it was enough to encourage two shepherds and one drippy-nosed angel to knock on his door. You could tell what they were because flannel bathrobes stuck out from under two jackets and silver garland peeked out from under the angel's toque. They jumped when the door cracked open. "Yes, what do you want," Mr. Hermit blurted, and the night air froze his words into a puff that obscured his face.

The tallest shepherd spoke, though he was very afraid. "We saw your light and thought you might help." He unzipped his jacket and reached inside. "After our pageant, we leave for a week. And the kennel is full." The shepherd held a tiny orange tabby kitten in his hand. "We found him freezing in the back alley. Can you please take care of him?"

Mr. Hermit took a step back. The smaller shepherd desperately piped up, "We'll pay you the thirty dollars we were going to give the kennel."

After what seemed like forever, Mr. Hermit said quietly, "Okay." The angel's face lit with joy as the shepherd handed the kitten over. Then the kids rushed off to their pageant.

MR. HERMIT SPENT THE EVENING trying to remember what a kitten needs. He made a litter box with the sand he normally used on sidewalks. He opened a can of tuna and he and the kitten shared it. After supper, when he watched the news on TV, the kitten sat on his lap and purred like a coffee grinder, so he had to turn up the volume.

WHEN HE WENT TO BED, he shut his door, but the kitten cried. He waited, but the mewling got louder and Mr. Hermit heaved his pillow at the door. The crying stopped for a moment, then resumed with an added note of panic. Under the bedroom door, two white paws stretched in, toes spread, needle claws raking the carpet. "I'll teach you a lesson," Mr. Hermit thought. He went to the door, bent down, and pinched a little paw. A startled moment later the coffee grinder rattled to life, and the little claws retracted. Sighing in defeat, Mr. Hermit opened the door. The little cat shot up onto the bed and curled into the warm dent on his pillow.

Mr. Hermit growled. "*Thirty Bucks.* That's your name now, you little stray. There's only thirty bucks between you and the cold alley you came from."

THE NEXT MORNING, THIRTY BUCKS was interested in everything Mr. Hermit did. The kitten perched on top of the computer. He enjoyed the TV shows Mr. Hermit watched, especially the fast moving hockey games. Mr. Hermit laughed when the little cat batted at the screen, trying to catch the puck. Thirty Bucks appreciated every scrap of food or bit of attention. He even sat beside the tub worriedly twitching his whiskers when Mr. Hermit took a bath. Thirty Bucks joyfully followed Mr. Hermit everywhere on Christmas Day and Mr. Hermit began to enjoy the company of the happy little cat.

ON BOXING DAY, IT WAS snowing big dry flakes when Mr. Hermit went to the grocery store to buy cat food. He was careful, but he didn't see Thirty Bucks scoot out into the snow behind him.

Shopping only took half an hour, but it was a very cold day. When he got home, Mr. Hermit saw paw prints in the snow and his heart felt like ice. Thirty Bucks was too skinny to stay warm for long. Worried, he followed the prints. They wandered across a neighbour's lawn, under a fence, around a swing set, over some firewood, and onto a deck at the back of a large house. Brushing snow off his shoulders, he rang the doorbell. A white haired woman came to the door with Thirty Bucks perched on her shoulder.

MR. HERMIT SOON FOUND HiMSELF at a kitchen table with a steaming cup of hot chocolate, a gingerbread man, and Mr. and Mrs. Smith. The Smiths peppered him with happy questions about his job, his home, and who might win the evening's hockey game. Mr. Hermit told them about how he had lived in the little white house for 50 years, and worked as an accountant. He was quiet for a moment when they asked about his family. "My wife died of cancer 10 years ago," he said. "We had no children, and I really don't know anyone except a few people at work."

"Well, you've met us now." Mr. Smith said. An hour later, Mr. Hermit left with Thirty Bucks in his pocket and an invitation to come back for dinner.

THIRTY BUCKS WASN'T DISCOURAGED BY his cold adventure. In fact, Mr. Hermit had a hard time keeping track of the energetic kitten. Every time he opened the door, Thirty Bucks was a fuzzy blur. He got out five more times that week, and Mr. Hermit became quite good at following footprints and meeting neighbours. In one week, he had dinner with the Smiths, he attended a junior hockey game with the man from the corner house, and he helped the woman across the street shovel her sidewalks. When he went to get Thirty Bucks from her house he found out she had a sprained ankle and could not shovel the walk herself.

A WEEK AFTER THE SHEPHERDS and angel first appeared, three children carrying packages approached the little white house. Its sidewalk and the sidewalks of the neighbouring houses were neatly swept clear of snow. The porch light was on and an orange tabby kitten gazed out onto the street from where open curtains revealed a living room full of warm light. The door opened before they could knock, and Mr. Hermit said, "Come in," at the same time as he expertly snagged a leaping kitten out of the air.

THE KIDS HAD HOT CHOCOLATE with Mr. Hermit.

They gave him gifts of home-made cookies and a fancy pine-scented candle, but he wouldn't accept the thirty dollars they brought to pay for kitten-sitting. He suggested they take the money to the blue house across the road. The woman with the sprained ankle, he said, had two jobs and two kids, and could use a bit of good news.

THAT'S WHERE I COME INTO the picture. My mom took the thirty dollars to the grocery store, while I played with the kitten and my three new friends. Later, we went over to say thank you to Mr. Herman. We all thought it was funny that his real name was Herman, not Hermit.

WE ARE ALL OLDER NOW, but every Christmas we still get together somewhere and tell the surprising story of how following in the footsteps of such an unexpected little gift changed us all.

CPSIA information can be obtained at www.ICGtesting.com
Printed in the USA
LVIW01n0852030915
452618LV00006B/14